Weekly Reader Children's Book Club presents

Sir Toby Jingle's Beastly Journey

story and pictures by Wallace Tripp

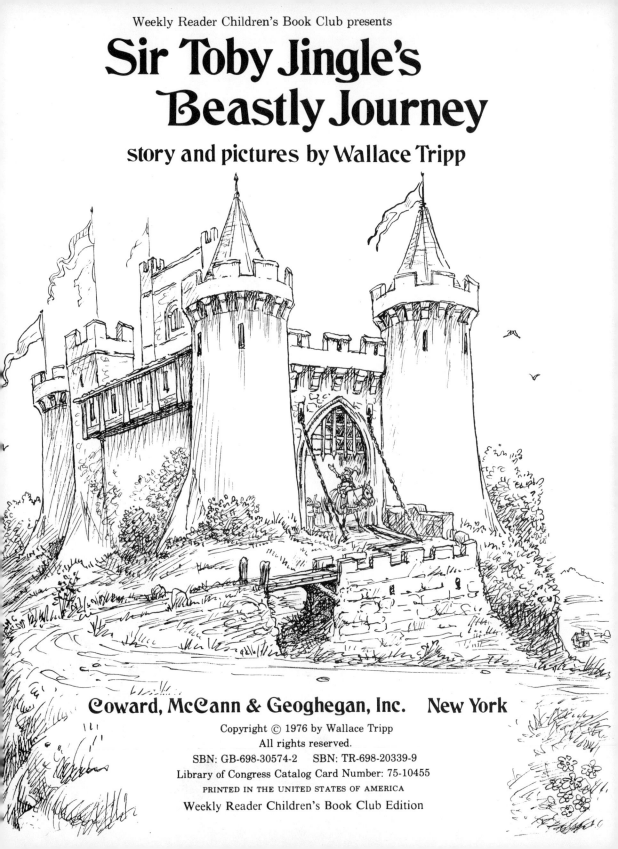

Coward, McCann & Geoghegan, Inc.   New York

SBN: GB-698-30574-2   SBN: TR-698-20339-9
Library of Congress Catalog Card Number: 75-10455
PRINTED IN THE UNITED STATES OF AMERICA
Weekly Reader Children's Book Club Edition

FOR BENJAMIN

Sir Toby Jingle was a knight who had done every brave thing from jabbing giants to trouncing trolls. Year after year ghastly creatures would slink out of Grimghast Forest and terrorize the peaceful villages. And year after year Sir Toby would send them howling and limping back.

In time the creatures came to think he had magical powers.

When he heard of these preposterous imaginings, Sir Toby would laugh, for he knew his success was due to the skill of long practice and his sharp wits, nothing more.

But as deed followed deed, year followed year, and Sir Toby found himself chasing the children and grandchildren of his early opponents.

His old bones began to tell him something.

One night Sir Toby studied his charts and maps of Grimghast Forest. He planned and thought.

Sir Toby at last fell off to sleep, ready for his last great adventure.

Early the next morning he was clip-clopping down the highway straight into Grimghast Forest.

"Eyes and ears wide open," said Sir Toby to his horse as they entered the dark wood. "We won't be meeting any friends today."

A short way into the forest he met two old enemies, a griffin and a bear. At the sight of Sir Toby they nearly jumped out of their skins.

"Ho! Ho! No need to be afraid, friends," said Sir Toby cheerfully. "Today I seek my fortune. Join me, and you shall have your fair share."

The two animals glared suspiciously at the knight. Then the griffin whispered to the bear, "Let's join him and slay him when he's off guard."

"Aye," agreed the bear. "This knight has laid low many a bear and griffin. This scar across my nose was his handiwork."

"Jingle clipped my wings when I was a dear, innocent little griflet. Revenge, I say."

And so they went on together.

They had not gone far when they met a dragon sunning on Skull Rock.

"Greetings," said Sir Toby. "My companions and I are seeking our fortune and would be glad of your jolly company."

The bear crept over to the dragon. "Join us, worm," she whispered, "and help us get revenge on this blasted knight."

"I certainly will," hissed the dragon, narrowing her eyes. "My kinsmen have many a score to settle with this tin soldier. This limp I have was the work of his sword."

And so the growing band continued.

The dragon told Sir Toby there was, not a bone's throw beyond, a deep cave containing a fortune in jewels.

"A fortune, you say!" exclaimed Sir Toby, who knew the cave as well as his own shoes. "This calls for a look."

Once the clatter of hooves had grown distant in the cave the animals rolled and pushed and piled stone on stone until the entrance was sealed forever.

Then the creatures ambled down the trail, congratulating one another for their cleverness.

Suddenly they heard a sound.

Three hearts stood still.

"Roaring radishes! No fortune in there, friends. I rode the whole length of the cave, and there's not a copper penny in the place."

"My, my," Sir Toby added as they traveled on, "you are an eager lot, getting ahead of me like this. But your enthusiasm shall not go unrewarded, I can tell you that."

About midafternoon the dusty and panting adventurers came upon a grim tiger picking his teeth with a splinter of bone.

"Good afternoon," called out Sir Toby. "Would you care to join our band of fortune hunters?"

The tiger squinted with his good eye. He looked from Sir Toby to the others, who, by winks and nods, urged the tiger to join them.

"That I will," he replied in an evil purr. "That I will."
And with a switch of his tail he joined the procession.

In due time Sir Toby reined in and dismounted. "A bite to eat and then to sleep, dear friends. Tomorrow our fortunes will be made," he said. "I promise you."

The brutes raced back to the campsite.
Suddenly, from behind there came a familiar sound.
"I'll be a two-tailed toad! I left to get us some berries, and look what's happened to my tin suit."

The next morning the band went on. Soon a fox shot past. An ogre was in hot pursuit. Sir Toby again invited an old enemy to join in the quest.

"He's the old sack who parted me from my three finger-bones," said the ogre. "Why haven't you gotten rid of him?"

"Easier said than done," replied the tiger.

"Makes himself invisible," said the dragon with a shudder.

"His magic sword sings aloud," mumbled the griffin.

"We'll see about that!" said the ogre, gnashing his teeth as he fell in line behind the others.

Soon they drew alongside the well. "Let us stop for a drink," called out the ogre.

CRAK!

PLIP.

The animals were about to make a meal of Sir Toby's horse when they heard that old familiar sound.

"Horns, thorns, and unicorns!" exclaimed Sir Toby. "Good thing I had hold of the bucket rope."

Soon the merry band emerged from the forest. Away down the sunny road they came to a castle. "Let us stop here to be sure of our directions, friends," said Sir Toby.

"After you, my friends," said smiling Sir Toby, closing the great gate, the gate of his own castle, behind him.

"In there, I think," he said, pointing through the courtyard door.

They charged for the door where Sir Toby stood, key in hand. He stepped back, shut the door, and locked it with a click.

They were trapped!

The beasts howled and carried on for a week.

But it wasn't long before they tired of pounding the door and howling and settled down.

And so it was the fortune of Sir Toby Jingle was made as people flocked from miles around to see—at only a penny, mind you—the finest zoo in the land.

The beastly bullies began to delight in the applause
of the crowd and put on a wonderful show.

And Sir Toby had plenty of time for his books and
gardens.